MORNING STAR, EVENING STAR, SUPERSTAR

A SHORT STORY

ALEXANDRIA BLAELOCK

BlueMere Books
MELBOURNE, AUSTRALIA

For permission requests, please contact
enquiries@bluemerebooks.com.

Ordering Information:
Discounts are available on quantity purchases. For details, contact orders@bluemerebooks.com.

Morning Star, Evening Star, Superstar/Alexandria Blaelock
paperback ISBN: 978-1-925749-37-3
digital ISBN: 978-1-925749-38-0

Book Layout © BookDesignTemplates.com

MORNING STAR, EVENING STAR, SUPERSTAR

Hunter Preston strode, buck naked, through the wide-open glass back doors of his house, stretched and roared in the Summer sunshine.

Then ran the last few steps across the stoned patio toward his sparkling clean swimming pool, jumped, and pulling his knees towards his chest, did a massive bombie into the pool.

Christy did a double-take and nearly fell out of her tree.

She scrabbled at the jacaranda's dry, scratchy bark, trying to keep her place. Grateful for the slight protection her threadbare jeans and long-sleeved t-shirt offered.

She looked through the view-finder again. Barracuda of the Business World indeed!

Quite a contrast from the urbane and sophisticated gentleman in perfectly fitted tux she'd photographed at last week's launch banquet.

Or the dark and dangerous man straddling his Ducati in tight blue jeans and a black leather jacket mid-week.

But not so different from yesterday's lithe and sporty footballer playing in the charity match.

She liked what she'd seen of him, not just physically, but the courteous way he interacted with people around him too.

As if he didn't think he was someone special.

And in the league of super-rich arseholes, that did make him someone special.

She sighed and leaned her forehead against the tree trunk.

She'd make more money selling these pictures to a nudie magazine, but even though she'd stooped as low as taking paparazzo style photos, she'd signed an exclusive contract and wasn't going to break it.

Though it wouldn't do his reputation any harm, and she could do with the extra money.

Freelancing was hard enough, what with photos of pretty much anything you like freely available on the Internet.

It was a sad indictment of the state of the world that the most reliable and well-paid work was private investigation.

And that's a dirty business at the best of times, so she wasn't going to make it any dirtier.

Not that she knew what was going to happen to her photos, but she trusted Mack not to get her into any sticky situations.

Hopefully, whoever was buying was going to respect Hunter's privacy and not on-sell them either.

But right now, she hoped he'd quickly retire to his million-dollar heritage-listed mansion so she could leave without detection.

Slight though she was, her precarious perch was uncomfortable, and the sight of his luscious body was making her light-headed.

Or maybe that was not having eaten breakfast.

Not to mention the thought of his lean, hard body against hers was making her heart race so fast she thought she might have a heart attack.

Though there wasn't much chance of him seeing her, let alone touching her.

She snapped off another couple of pictures, tempted to keep one or two for herself.

There's no harm in dreaming about what you can't have. And he'd be a great addition to her vision board.

But even if she could have him, there's no way he'd slot neatly into her life.

Even if he wanted to.

She heard a slight noise and looked down. It was a big fluffy golden retriever snuffling around the base of the tree. It looked up at her and whined softly.

More likely he'd dominate her life, and she'd find herself slotting into his.

Like this cutie.

"Nice doggy, go away."

It wagged its tail.

"Go away," she hissed, making shooing motions, "I don't want Him over here, checking what you're doing."

It jumped on its hind legs bracing its body against the tree and woofed up at her.

A quick glance assured her that Hunter, sporting in the pool, hadn't yet noticed his dog's preoccupation, so she risked leaning over to scratch its head.

Too late she realised she was slipping and grappled frantically with thin air to save herself.

She crashed to the ground, fortunately, cushioned by a lush manicured lawn, the breath leaving her lungs in a whoosh.

There was no time to recover, for the dog was on her, trying to crawl through her arms to lick her face.

She rolled over to escape it and heard the sickening crunch as she crushed her camera before she felt the stab of pain.

She gave in and let the dog lick her.

Now she had no camera, and the fate of the SD card was doubtful. Would there be any salvageable images?

This was what happened when you got greedy.

It wasn't very professional to break your equipment while being tickled to death by a dog.

Squeezing her eyes shut to hold back the tears she thought of all the bills waiting to be paid.

She was so tired of struggling.

"Biscuit, what do you think you are doing?"

The dog backed up and sat down, leaving her a clear view of Hunter's strong, square face.

His crystal blue eyes seemed to bore right through her and out the other side.

Not the most comfortable thought.

"Ah, another tourist who got lost."

He leaned down and grabbed her hand, pulling her to her feet, less roughly than she'd expected.

He held her hand for a fraction of a second too long as he continued his intense searching look.

Did she have something on her face?

She dragged her forearm across her face just in case.

He grinned down at her, revealing even white teeth, then nonchalantly brushed a few flecks of grass off her shoulders.

The small towel draped demurely around his waist, emphasised his slim hips and highlighted rows of muscles on muscles on muscles.

Not really a barracuda.

More like a puma, trussed up for its visit with the zoo vet.

He flicked his damp hair off his face with a toss of his head.

"I can see you're a photographer, but who are you, and why are you here?"

She squared her shoulders and stood as tall as she could to minimise their height difference.

Under other circumstances, she'd fit snugly under his arm, but she tried to banish the thought and concentrate on the conversation.

"My name is Christy Zachary, and I'm with Underground Investigations."

"Christy Zachary, hmmmmmm...

"Didn't you do a spread about street kids a few years ago?"

"Um, well, yes."

She was surprised he remembered it. It'd been a big thing, quickly dropped in favour of more pleasant topics.

"Times are obviously hard if you're in investigations."

"Well..."

"Okay, who sent you?"

"I don't know, I just take the pictures."

"Probably just my ex-wife then," he gave her a crocodile smile.

"Do you have enough pictures, or would you like me to pose for some more?"

His hands slipped down towards the towel.

She blushed and backed away, waving her hands as a barrier in front of her, "no no no, thanks, I'm fine."

"Oh look, you broke your camera. Maybe we should schedule for a more suitable time, when you have your spare."

"No, really, it'll be fine."

"Well, come along then, and I'll show you out. Unless you'd care to climb the fence again?"

She crouched to pick up the pieces of her camera, hoping she could salvage some of it and tried not to catch his smiling eyes as he looked over his shoulder to make sure she was following.

What exactly did he find amusing about this situation?

There was clearly a lot more to him than the domineering businessman portrayed by the press.

Soon enough she was on the other side of the fence, slightly consoled by Biscuit's lingering kiss.

She ignored the security guard and leant on the wall trying to catch her breath.

Well, trying not to cry actually.

The pieces in her arms were her spare camera, and she couldn't afford to buy another.

And you can't be a photographer if you don't have the tools of the trade.

《《 • 》》

Somehow Hunter managed to get back inside the house before he started laughing.

Christy Zachary, currently from Underground Investigations, was like an adorably angry kitten. Green eyes wide, arched back, black hair on end, hissing.

He wanted to play that kitten game where you try to tickle her belly without getting scratched, but he had the feeling he'd have to be pretty fast.

Grabbing a beer from the fridge on the way, he stripped off his towel and went back outside to sunbake on it.

Biscuit climbed up on the lounger, and after turning in a circle, lay down at his feet with her chin on his ankle.

Christy Zachary couldn't be that bad if his cranky old dog liked her.

And now that he thought about it, what was that stupid magazine that wanted to run a story on him? Man something?

He'd insist they use her.

He eased himself out from under Biscuit and went to make a few calls.

《《 • 》》

Back in her empty apartment, Christy discovered neither the lense nor the camera could be saved.

Though she managed to pull a few pics from the card and get them off to Mack with some of the previous.

That at least would bring a few hundred in.

Which would help, because she'd already sold everything of value, including her best cameras.

She still had her phone, of course, and those pictures would be fine for some kinds of jobs.

But the fancy camera was not just a tool of trade, it was a credential too.

In the meantime, she checked to find no new orders and no suitable new jobs. She crossed her fingers and sent off a few overdue account emails because that was at least doing something.

If her life continued along this vein, it wouldn't be long before she'd have to start redefining her hard nos.

Or reconsider life as a supermarket checkout chick.

She flopped on the couch, pulled her pink plaid blanket up to her chin and spent the next few days sleeping to escape from her problems.

She knew she had to do something, but she couldn't bear to think about it.

Something would happen to save her; she just didn't know what yet.

«« • »»

Hunter knocked again on the weathered apartment door. So hard he thought it might come off its hinges. If she didn't answer soon, he wasn't sure what he was going to do.

He was just about to knock again when it opened a crack to reveal Christy's squinting eye half covered by a tousled lock of black hair in some kind of anime cuteness.

After a moment, when she didn't say anything, he pushed the door open to reveal a small dishevelled woman in a stained oversize t-shirt. One who'd clearly just got off the shabby little couch.

Which was a little funny given how much time he'd spent changing his clothes in the hopes of impressing her.

Google had been surprisingly unhelpful on the topic of what to wear to commission an artist.

And now that he was here, the charcoal suit matched with a white and blue striped shirt, socks and tie, plus gleaming white gold accessories seemed a bit overdone.

Especially given that the couch was one of two pieces of furniture in the tiny but neat studio apartment, the other being a low table.

Dammit, why did she make him feel a teenager who was trying too hard?

"Nice place you have here."

Christy snorted and rubbed the sleep from her eyes.

He held out a gift-wrapped box, "I bought you a new camera."

She didn't look at the box, just screwed her eyes up to look at him, perhaps seeking a different f/stop.

"I don't know what to say."

He grinned, "thank you would be a good start."

"Oh, sorry," she blushed and looked away, "thank you very much."

"That's better. Now you ask me if I'd like some coffee."

She filled an old kettle with water and turned it on before rinsing some chipped cups from the drainer and spooning instant coffee into the cups.

She didn't look like much of a morning person, and he wondered whether he might have been better off bringing her coffee than a camera.

"You don't believe much in worldly goods, do you?"

"I'm not here much, not that it's any of your business."

"But it is, I'm a prospective employer."

She made a face after sniffing the milk and put it back in the tiny fridge on the bench.

"I was quite impressed by your street life spread, and some of your other work. You've a knack for bringing out the best in your subjects.

"And when *Metropolitan Man* magazine approached me for an interview, I said I wouldn't do it unless you took the pictures."

The kettle clicked off, so she poured the water into the cups, offering him black with no sugar before taking a sip of her own.

"You're insane, they'll never agree."

"They already did. They'll be in touch shortly."

Somewhere her phone rang with a cartoon theme tune he vaguely recognised before cutting out.

"Seeing as you don't currently have a camera, it seemed a good idea to get you one."

"What? How did you know that?"

"Well, in my position a few discreet enquiries are in order."

"But why me?"

He put the cup on the table without taking a sip.

"Leaving aside your undeniable talent, you won't be obtrusive, and if anyone notices you, you'll look good following me around.

"But—"

"Look, all you have to do is follow me around taking photos, it's what you've been doing for the last few weeks after all."

"Yes, but-"

He looked at his watch, "I've got to get to the office now, but one of my assistants will be here shortly to give you a hand with your wardrobe selection."

"But—"

"Good, I'm glad that's settled." He shook her limp hand, "I'll see you later this afternoon."

And then he left, trying to smother his self-satisfied smile.

That went better than expected.

He couldn't wait to see if she arrived.

《《 • 》》

Oh.

My.

God.

As if the lingering scent of Hunter's woody cologne wasn't enough, now she was trying to wrangle Justin, the immaculately turned out Queer Eye.

Who'd gone all bug-eye.

His horror at the state of her wardrobe, more empty capsule than wardrobe, must surely be audible six blocks away.

Any minute now her downstairs neighbours would be banging on their roof with a broomstick to tell her to quieten down.

Not that he was squawking for nothing.

It was some time since she'd had the kind of well-paid open and above-board gigs that required decent clothes rather than undercover work up trees and behind parked cars.

And damn him, Justin was right, she was on a downward spiral.

And something needed to be done.

And yes, new clothes were an investment in her future.

She allowed herself to be dragged to the waiting limousine with the minimum of protest, mainly because she was trying to calculate the maximum she could afford to spend.

Their first stop was a shoe store where he chose some ridiculously expensive black ballet flats for her to try on.

"They're beautiful," she breathed, "but way too expensive."

"Try walking around. Are they comfortable? "Do they rub?"

She walked a few paces then crouched, and stretched, and climbed on the chairs.

"They're fine. Perhaps perfect."

"So, after an eight-hour day of following and photographing Mr Preston, you'll still be standing?"

Christy bounced a couple of times to try them out, "yes, I think so. But I can't afford them."

"Goodness, were you not listening when I talked about investing in yourself?"

"Yes, but—"

Justin pulled a plain black credit card from his back pocket and waggled it in her face. "Mr Preston has authorised me to cover your reasonable expenses for your assignment."

"These shoes, delightful as they are, are not reasonable expenses."

"Christy, Christy, Christy," he said, shaking his head. "In this instance, I am the sole arbiter of what are reasonable expenses, and I will brook no argument from you."

She made another feeble attempt at protest, and he dragged her to a nearby full-length mirror.

And pointed at the woman who looked as though she'd just crawled out from underneath a newspaper blanket behind a commercial rubbish skip.

"Take a long hard look at yourself woman."

He took his phone from his jacket pocket and opened a calendar app. "This week alone, Mr Preston has three board meetings, a government consultative committee, a TV interview, and a charity dinner at a high-end hotel.

"Are you telling me this vagrant," he gestured at the mirror, "will be permitted to enter any of these places?"

She made a doubtful face.

"Do you have any concept of the harm you could do to his reputation dressing like a tramp and trailing around after him trying to take his picture?"

She winced as his barbs drove home and shook her head.

"And what about your reputation?"

She shrunk a little smaller.

"Will you accept my judgement in this matter?"

She nodded.

Justin, fully vindicated, smiled beatifically, and pulled out another couple of pairs of shoes for her to try.

Over the next few hours, she followed him from store to store, tried on all the clothes and lingerie he offered and accepted his verdict without comment.

The black card got such a workout she wondered how it wasn't smoking.

She didn't complain when he took her to an upmarket Japanese restaurant for lunch.

Or when he left her at a Beauty Salon for a massage and makeover. Or when he told her what to put on when she was done.

And when she couldn't find the clothes she'd arrived in, she decided not to ask.

《《 • 》》

At first, Hunter didn't notice the woman taking photographs.

She discreetly drifted around the floor, pointing her camera down corridors, at windows and him.

He only noticed her because he was on the phone, staring through his glass office wall, and she happened to be the only thing moving at the time.

It took him a moment to recognise the elegant woman in skinny black jeans, a lightly fitted black silk shirt, flat black shoes, and a long silver chain.

As she turned her head, he saw her hair was caught up in a loose bun held together by chopsticks, and he wanted to pull them out and thread his fingers through it as he kissed her.

So intensely, she'd forget everything else.

She wasn't an angry kitten anymore; she'd become something infinitely more beautiful and much more dangerous; a black panther.

Even worse, a panther he'd invited to stalk and capture him.

The call ended, but he kept the phone at his ear, an excuse to watch her slowly raise her camera to her face and press the shutter release in his direction.

God help him.

Would the pictures show how incredibly attractive he found her?

He licked his lips.

Would there be a difference now they both knew who the buyer was?

《《 • 》》

She felt weirdly sexy in her black photographer's outfit. Or maybe sexy wasn't the right word, maybe it was confident.

Capable.

In control

Bold.

She locked eyes with Hunter as she raised the camera towards him.

The world shrunk to his tiny image reflected in the window.

He licked his lips and turned to face her.

She heard something break inside her.

Was it her self-control?

She took a few shots.

Maybe she wasn't in control, maybe she was just shameless.

She lowered the camera and took a step towards his office.

He put the phone down and rose from his chair.

Still meeting her eyes.

Maybe being dominated by him wouldn't be so bad if that was what it took to feel like a sexy grown-the-hell-up woman.

She took another step, and he walked around his desk.

How long before he left her a puddle of mush as he walked away looking for someone more exciting than her?

Did it matter?

At least he wouldn't take all her cash with him when he left.

She'd be left with money in the bank, clothes in her closet, and a corridor of doors opening in his wake.

Another step brought her to his office door.

He sat on the edge of his desk, waiting to see what she'd do next.

What the hell, she'd think of reasons why not later.

She stepped into the room, shutting the door behind her and leaning on it.

He pointed a remote to trigger the privacy frosting, then walked over to kiss her.

Thoroughly.

Deeply.

As if she was the only woman on the planet.

The kiss was better than he'd imagined.

And Christy didn't scratch him.

Her soft, warm body seemed to melt into his, and her hair, when he set it free was smooth and silky as it slid through his fingers. He was drowning in her light floral fragrance.

How could one woman have snared him so completely with so little effort?

He broke off the kiss, but she stood on tiptoe to capture him again.

This was no good, he had to tell her the truth before it got out of hand. He gently pushed her away.

"There's almost nothing I'd rather do than be kissed senseless by you, but I have a confession to make."

She looked up at him from dazed eyes.

He groaned and forced himself to guide her across to the conversational side of his office where he sat her on a couch and poured her a glass of water.

She took a couple of sips and seemed better able to string together coherent thoughts, which was more than he could say for himself.

He turned his back on her, and paced the length of his office, trying to work out how to tell her.

An action that seemed to annoy her as she snapped, "All right, out with it."

And given he'd been a hair's breadth from losing control and devouring her on the couch she sat on, it seemed a reasonable response.

"Argh." he started.

"I knew who you were all along, and I was the one who hired you to take the pictures of me."

She looked at him, took a sip of water, and put the glass down on the coffee table.

He didn't know if she was thinking, or trying to say something, or just wondering if he was some kind of stalker psycho.

"I just wanted to meet you, and it seemed like there was no other way."

He felt like he was losing his edge, so he flopped on the couch beside her and took her hand.

"Why aren't you saying anything?"

"Well, it's not like you've given me much of an opportunity yet."

"What are you thinking?"

She scratched her head, "I'm just wondering when, and how, and why me."

"Okay, well, um, you're an amazing artist, and I love your work, and I wanted to meet you, and when I found out you weren't taking commissions or doing events, I did some research and found out that hiring the investigator was about the only way I could hire you, and maybe meet you, and I thought I'd just book in and see what happened and maybe—"

He forced his mouth to close before he could look like even more of an idiot than he already did.

And when he dared to meet her eyes, they were dancing, she snorted, "Barracuda of the Business World indeed."

He smiled a little, and when he realised he still had her hand, a little more.

"Are you seriously telling me you've gone as giddy as a school girl because you're meeting me?"

He giggled.

Oh my god he giggled!

What the hell was wrong with him?

She laughed.

And laughed and laughed.

And when it seemed like she couldn't laugh any more, took a deep breath and gasped, "I'm sorry," before laughing some more.

Fanning her red face with her spare hand.

And when she could breathe again, she grabbed his face and kissed him.

"Let's get out of here," she said.

Christy lay on a lounger, reading the *Metropolitan Man* article, Biscuit by her side.

With a whoop, Hunter bolted from the house and landed with an enormous splash in the pool.

She lowered the magazine to watch him swim back towards her and crawl up the stairs to shake the water off on her.

Biscuit growled half-heartedly and retreated back into the house.

She smiled up at him, wondering which of them had been more nervous about meeting the big celebrity other.

He eased into the vacant space beside her and dropped a kiss on her lips.
Not that it mattered anymore, they'd met, and all that remained was the rest of their lives.

THE END

ABOUT THE AUTHOR

Alexandria Blaelock writes stories, some of them for *Ellery Queen's Mystery Magazine* and *Pulphouse Fiction Magazine*. She's also written four self-help books applying business techniques to personal matters like getting dressed, cleaning house, and feeding your friends.

As a recovering Project Manager, she's probably too fond of sticking to plan. She lives in a forest because she enjoys birdsong, the scent of gum leaves and the sun on her face. When not telecommuting to parallel universes from her Melbourne based imagination, she watches K-dramas, talks to animals, and drinks Campari. At the same time.

Discover more at www.alexandriablaelock.com.

OTHER SHORT STORIES BY ALEXANDRIA BLAELOCK

Alma's Grace
Balancing the Book
Bygone Boyfriend
Carmelita Basingstoke
Fate in Your Hands
Kiss of Death
Lady of the Looking Glass
Life in the Security Directorate
Long Weekend in the Snow
Love in the Security Directorate
Morning Star, Evening Star, Superstar
Needy Bitch
Payton's Run
Phoenix Child
Secret Singer
Shining Star
Ship in a Bottle
Simone Says Hands in the Air
The Day the Schedule Broke
The Guardian's Vigil
Toy Soldiers

BOOKS BY ALEXANDRIA BLAELOCK

FICTION

That Love Nonsense

MS BLAELOCK'S BOOKS

Stress Free Dinner Parties
Signature Wardrobe Planning
Holistic Personal Finance
Minimally Viable Housekeeping

www.ingramcontent.com/pod-product-compliance
Lightning Source LLC
Chambersburg PA
CBHW070455170726
48291CB00005B/1766